LADYBIRD BOOKS

UK | USA | Canada | Ireland | Australia | India | New Zealand | South Africa
Ladybird Books is part of the Penguin Random House group of companies
whose addresses can be found at global.penguinrandomhouse.com.

www.penguin.co.uk   www.puffin.co.uk   www.ladybird.co.uk

Penguin
Random House
UK

This book was previously published as *The Big Tale of Little Peppa* in 2014
This edition published 2017
001

This book copyright © Astley Baker Davies Ltd/Entertainment One UK Ltd 2014, 2017
Adapted by Mandy Archer

This book is based on the TV series *Peppa Pig*.
Peppa Pig is created by Neville Astley and Mark Baker.
Peppa Pig © Astley Baker Davies Ltd/Entertainment One UK Ltd 2003.
www.peppapig.com

Printed in China

A CIP catalogue record for this book is available from the British Library

ISBN: 978-0-241-32716-6

All correspondence to:
Ladybird Books, Penguin Random House Children's
80 Strand, London WC2R 0RL

The Tale of Little PePPa

Once upon a time, Peppa's best friend, Suzy Sheep, came to play.

"I've got something to show you," said Suzy.

"Look!"

"It's me," said Suzy.

"You're not a baby, Suzy," said Peppa, shaking her head.

"This is an **old** photo," Suzy explained. "It was taken when I was little."

Peppa snorted. Suzy was being

very silly today!

Suzy pointed at Peppa. "In the olden days you were a baby too!" she said.

"No, I wasn't!"
said Peppa.

"Yes, you were,"
insisted Suzy.
"Ask your mummy."

Peppa and Suzy raced inside. Mummy Pig was working on the computer.

"Mummy!" cried Peppa. "Suzy is making up stories!"

"No, I'm not," Suzy said crossly.
Peppa told Mummy Pig about Suzy's silly idea that they used to be babies.

"But you **WERE** a baby, Peppa!" said Mummy Pig.

Mummy Pig took a look on the computer.
"Who do you think this is, Peppa?" Mummy Pig asked.
Peppa thought that the baby looked a bit like her cousin.
"Is it Baby Alexander?" she asked.

"No!" replied Mummy Pig.
"That's **you** as a baby, Peppa."

Hee! Hee!

Hee! Hee!

Suzy and Peppa giggled.
They'd never seen Baby Peppa before!

George and Daddy Pig came in to see what all the fuss was about.

"Look, Daddy!" said Peppa. "That's me as a baby!"

"I remember it," said Daddy Pig. "That photo was taken on our first day in this house."

"What do you mean?" asked Peppa.

Daddy Pig told Peppa, Suzy and George that they had moved into their house when Peppa was very little.

"We brought all our things on the top of our car," he said.

"Mummy Pig put some pictures up," said Daddy Pig.

"Daddy Pig put up a shelf . . ." said Mummy Pig.

". . . and Grandpa Pig made us a lovely flower garden!" she continued.

Peppa and Suzy went outside to see what
Grandpa Pig's lovely flower garden
looked like now.

It had completely

disappeared!

"Daddy Pig looked after the flower garden," sighed Mummy Pig.

"Er . . ." said Daddy Pig, "we had the wrong kind of soil for flowers."

"Was Suzy my friend in the olden days?" asked Peppa.
Daddy Pig nodded. "Of course!" he said.

Hee! Hee!

"You and Suzy have always been **best friends.**"

Peppa wondered what games she played with Suzy when they were little.

"Did we jump up and down in muddy puddles?"

"No, Peppa," laughed
Mummy Pig. "You were babies.
You couldn't even walk!"

"What did we do when we were babies, Mrs Pig?" asked Suzy.

"You cried . . .

you burped . . .

and you laughed!"

Suzy and Peppa burst out laughing.

Hee! Hee!

Hee! Hee!

"Baby Peppa!"

"Baby Suzy!"

"Then you grew into toddlers," continued Mummy Pig.
"But where was George?" Peppa asked.

"He was a baby in my
tummy!"
said Mummy Pig.

George looked very surprised at this part of the story. What a funny idea!

Peppa thought for a minute. Daddy's tummy was even bigger than Mummy's. "Is there a baby in there?" she said.

"No, Peppa," chuckled Daddy Pig.

"This tummy is *pure muscle!*"

Mummy Pig said that, after a little while, George was born.

And she remembered the time that Granny and Grandpa Pig gave George a very special present.

"Can you guess what it was, Peppa?"

Peppa knew straight away.

"Mr Dinosaur!"

she cried.

Daddy Pig explained that Peppa and
Suzy didn't stay little for very long.

They liked to jump...

Hee!

Hee!

La la la!

and **run** around all over the place.

and **dance**...

Snort!

Snort!

La la la!

"Then one day," said Mummy Pig, "you saw something amazing ..."

"...a muddy

puddle!"

Mummy Pig said, "You loved jumping **up** and **down** in muddy puddles."

After Mummy and Daddy Pig's big tale of little Peppa, Suzy, George and Peppa ran outside into the garden.

"I still love muddy puddles!"

Splash!

Peppa cheered and jumped into the biggest one she could find. Suzy and George jumped in, too.

Daddy Pig went to find the camera.
"Let's take a photo of you now," he suggested.

Peppa, Suzy and George did their **best smiles**.

Click!

Little or big, Peppa will always love jumping up and down in

muddy puddles!